Wilde Ride

WITHDRAWN FROM STOCK
KU-555-771

Read more about the Wilde Family in ...

Wilde Day Out
Wilde Style
Running Wilde
Wilde Child
Wilde Party

Other series by Jenny Oldfield:

Definitely Daisy
Totally Tom
Horses of Half-Moon Ranch
My Little Life
Home Farm Twins
The Dreamseeker Trilogy

The WILDE FAMILY

Wilde Ride

by Jenny Oldfield

illustrated by Sarah Nayler

Hodder Children's Books
a division of Hodder Headline Limited

Thanks to all the *wild* kids who have told me jokes and funny stories during my visits to schools and libraries

Text copyright © Jenny Oldfield 2004
Illustrations copyright © Sarah Nayler 2004

ST. MARY'S ROAD
BRANCH

First published in Great Britain in 2004
by Hodder Children's Books

The right of Jenny Oldfield and Sarah Nayler to be identified as the Author and Illustrator respectively of the Work has been asserted by them in accordance with the Copyright, Designs and Patents Act 1988.

10 9 8 7 6 5 4 3 2 1

All rights reserved. No part of this publication may be reproduced, stored in a retrieval system, or transmitted in any form or by any means without the prior written permission of the publisher, nor be otherwise circulated in any form of binding or cover other than that in which it is published and without a similar condition being imposed on the subsequent purchaser.

All characters in this publication are fictitious, and any resemblance to real persons, living or dead, is purely coincidental.

A Catalogue record for this book is available from the British Library.

356555

ISBN 0 340 87322 1

Printed and bound in Great Britain by Bookmarque Ltd, Croydon, Surrey

The paper and board used in this paperback by Hodder Children's Books are natural recyclable products made from wood grown in sustainable forests. The manufacturing processes conform to the environmental regulations of the country of origin.

Hodder Children's Books
a division of Hodder Headline Ltd
338 Euston Road
London NW1 3BH

One

'Bummer!' Kayleigh Wilde slammed down her brush in disgust then ran her hands through her sticky, light brown hair. The article in *Teen Dream* made it look easy-peasy, but in real life getting the full volume curls she wanted was proving well hard.

'What's French for bummer?' her sister, Krystal, asked. She was practising for their summer holiday in Normandy. 'Like, boomère! Or what?'

Kayleigh ignored her. 'I'm bored!' she groaned. Her hair wouldn't behave itself, and she'd read her magazine from cover to cover. In the background, the radio played Cappucino's latest top ten hit, 'Dream Baby'.

'Boomère!' Krystal cried, dashing up to the mirror and pushing Kayleigh out of the way. She sprayed her fringe with volumizer and frizzed it up on end. 'Is that cool, or what?'

'Not!' Kayleigh snatched the can away. 'This stuff costs the earth, I'll have you know!'

'Dream baby, dream all day long, I'll sing you this sweet song, So you can dree-eeam!' Cappucino warbled.

'Girls, girls!' Maria Wilde, their mum, passed by Kayleigh's bedroom door carrying a stack of clean towels. 'You can help me with the ironing if you can't find anything better to do.'

'Da-dah, dream baby!' Kayleigh and Krystal sang along together, taking no notice.

'Carmel, how about you?' their mum asked, poking her head around the twins' door. 'Have you got time to help with the laundry?'

'Can't. Homework. Due in tomorrow!' Suddenly Carmel's English essay was mega important. 'How d'you spell catastrophe?' she asked.

'C-a-t-a-s ...'

'Hang on. C-a-t ... ?'

'Look it up,' Maria sighed, shaking her head and stacking the towels in the landing cupboard. Downstairs, baby Kyle beat his spoon against the tray of his high chair.

'Dream baby, of the sweetest things, I will give you diamond rings, So you can dree-eeam!' Kayleigh and Krystal chorused as their mum ran downstairs.

At the end of the track, the DJ came on the radio. 'That was Cappuccino with their 1980 hit, 'Dream Baby', and this is Melinda Swift bringing you raves from the grave for the next thirty minutes. But first the news with Eddie Norman ...'

'How d'you spell catastrophe?'

Carmel put down her pen and went next door into Kayleigh's room. 'That's *so* not cool!' she frowned at Krystal's frizzed fringe.

'It's OK, don't get your knickers in a twist!' Krystal took Kayleigh's brush and brushed savagely. 'It wasn't meant to be serious. I was messing around.'

'Yeah, with my spray!' Kayleigh muttered.

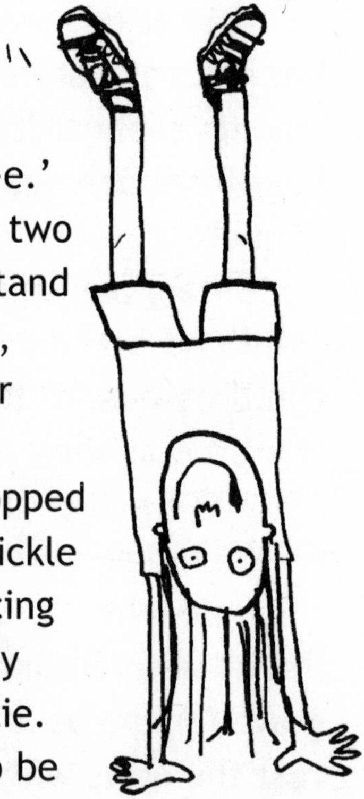

'C-a-t-a-s-t-r-o-p-h-e.' Jade bounded upstairs two at a time, did a handstand against Kayleigh's wall, then walked out on her hands.

Carmel's mouth dropped open. 'Hey, you're an ickle kid!' she objected, racing after Jade. 'You're only nine, and you like footie. You're not supposed to be spelling big words!'

'Waa-aaagh!' Kyle cried angrily for his supper.

Jade turned the right way up. 'I overheard you pestering Mum, so I asked Deanne for you,' she explained, as if that was OK then.

'B-b-but!' Carmel spluttered. She stared over the banister at their little sister, Deanne. 'She's seven!'

'Yeah, and a genius,' Jade reminded her. 'She reads all that stuff about planets and stars, remember.'

Deanne beamed. 'There was a catastrophe on Buggle-mug's home planet,' she reminded them. 'There was a ginormous fire and the green rock heated up until it was too hot for him to live there. That's how come he came to earth to stay with us!'

'Yeah, right!' Carmel said hastily at the mention of Deanne's invisible friend, Buggle-mug.

'And now, all you funky folk at home, get calling on 06818 655655!' Melinda burbled over the airwaves. 'Answer a few simple questions on pop trivia, and you can win a day out with a celeb! Yeah, that's right; you could be one phone call away from wending your way through the Tunnel of Lurve with the guy or gal of your dreams!' Music played, Kyle screamed.

'Did you hear that?' Krystal demanded. 'You can win a prize on the radio! All you have to do is call!'

'Yeah, you and six million others,' Carmel told her. She wrote the first three letters of 'catastrophe' on the palm of her hand. 'What comes after 't'?' she asked.

Kayleigh sighed and began throwing her weight around. 'Look, would you all just get out of my room!' she screeched. 'I've got a ton of homework to do, even if you haven't!'

'She's studying for a GCSE in Nail Painting!' Carmel sniggered, scarpering fast.

Kayleigh threw the brush and hit Krystal. The door slammed and she was left in peace.

'That's 06818 655 655!' Melinda reminded her. 'For a fun-filled trip this Saturday to Sundown Adventure Park!'

0-6-8-1-8. Krystal punched in the numbers.

'Did you check with Mum?' Carmel asked, spying over her shoulder. They'd just finished ham, chips, eggs and yucky green beans for supper, and Krystal had snuck off to grab the phone.

'Yep,' Krystal retorted. 6-5-5-6-5-5, she completed her call.

...y will you get on the ...amme!' Carmel scoffed. 'Zillions ... people want to win a day trip to Sundown!'

'Ssshh!' Krystal warned.

Sundown, with its statue of giant pigs standing on a hillside overlooking the theme park. The pigs were pink with black dots and very shiny. They scared passing motorists but were a famous landmark. Sundown, with its water-splashes and dicing-with-death rides. Carmel's eyes glowed. In spite of herself, she warmed to the idea of Krystal entering the competition. 'If there's two tickets, bags you take me!' she cried.

'Hello, this is the Mellow Out With Melinda Evening Show,' a voice said.

Krystal jumped so far she almost dropped the phone. 'Hi, I want to enter the competition,' she gabbled.

'Age?' the voice said.

'What? Oh, I'm eleven.'

'Liar!' Carmel hissed. They were both ten. Krystal was ten minutes older than her, worse luck. Boomère!

'Then the prize will be a family ticket.' The woman on the end of the phone sounded bored, like she'd said it a thousand times already. 'Give me your name and phone number, and we'll get back to you if you get drawn out of the hat.'

'I'm Krystal Wilde. Who's the celeb?'

'Krystal. How do you spell that?'

'K-r-y-s-t-a-l. Who's the celeb that we get to go on the rides with?' she insisted.

'What? Oh, we're not revealing that yet. Listen, can you hang up now and give others a chance to use the phone?' The woman hustled her into ending the call.

Carmel and Krystal frowned. 'Well, I guess that's the end of that,' Carmel muttered.

'It would've been cool,' Krystal insisted, accepting that the chances of being called back were practically zilch. 'I can answer on pop trivia better than anyone in our class. Go on – test me!'

But Carmel shook her head. No way. Krystal was already bigheaded enough about the Top Twenty and Top of the Pops. In fact, in her day-glo strappy T-shirts and trainers with reflective strips, she seemed to think she was a pop star!

The twins were about to forget the whole Sundown competition thing when suddenly Kayleigh arrived with a fresh update. 'Guess who the celeb is!' she enthused. 'It's gonna be Monty from Stateside. Y'know – Monty Del Sarto!'

Carmel's frown deepened. 'Never heard of him.'

'That's 'cos you're thick!' Kayleigh scoffed. 'Monty Del Sarto's big news. His pic's in the centrefold of this week's *Teen Dream*. You know him, don't you, Krystal?'

Krystal nodded. 'He's fit,' she

admitted. 'But hey, I'm never gonna get on to that radio quiz, so calm down.'

'Yeah, calm down!' Carmel echoed. 'Krystal's got about as much chance of winning that prize as ...' (she noticed Deanne come out of the kitchen holding hands with her invisible friend) '... as Buggle-mug has!'

'Take no notice!' Deanne whispered to him. 'They're only jealous!' She floated upstairs with a wide smile, whispering secrets and holding an invisible hand.

Wearily Krystal raised her eye-brows. 'That kid!' was all she said.

Then Jade burst out of the kitchen,

her mouth still full of chocolate cheesecake. 'Melinda's giving away twenty tickets to Sundown!' she spluttered. 'A kid called Simon just won three of them. He gets to ride The Wave with Monty!'

Carmel was speechless. Woah, The Wave! That was the ride where you sat in a tiny yellow boat and faced a wall of water. You looked up for ever and all you saw was this liquid wall. Then, as the boat rose, the wave curled at the top and came crashing down towards you. It swallowed up the boat, which rocked like crazy and you got soaked through and came out at the top. It was wild.

'Wicked!' Kayleigh sighed. Getting down with Monty!

'Dream on, baby!' Krystal muttered, by now convinced that the phone would never ring.

Brrring-brrring!

Krystal, Carmel, Kayleigh and Jade jumped a mile.

Brrriiing!

'Will someone please answer that!' Mum yelled from the kitchen.

Krystal stared at Kayleigh, who edged towards the phone.

'Quick!' Carmel gasped. 'Pick it up.'

Gingerly Kayleigh lifted the receiver. 'Hello,' she mumbled suspiciously.

Carmel and Krystal rushed forward to crush her against the wall. 'Who is it?' they whispered.

'No ... yes ... hang on a sec,' Kayleigh said slowly into the phone. Then she handed it over to Krystal. 'It's for you!' she hissed.

With trembling fingers, Krystal held it to her ear.

'This is the Melinda Evening Show,' said the same bored voice as before.

Krystal took a deep breath but said nothing.

'Your name has come up. Are you ready to answer some questions?'

'Yes,' Krystal whispered. About as

ready as she would be to dash into a blazing building! All of a sudden, she felt that everything she knew about pop trivia could be written on the back of a postage stamp.

'Are you on air?' Carmel hissed. 'Go for it, Krystal!'

Krystal stamped on her foot to keep her quiet.

'Mum, Krystal's gonna be on the radio!' Kayleigh yelled at the top of her voice.

The kitchen door flew open and Mum emerged carrying Kyle. Behind her, the radio continued to play raves from the grave. Upstairs, Deanne appeared on the landing with Buggle-mug, while down in the hallway, Jade gave Carmel a whoop and a high-five.

'I want you to stay on the

line,' the woman told Krystal. 'The next voice you hear will be Melinda's. She'll ask you the questions. If you get them right, she gives you the prize while you're still on air. Is that clear?'

'Yes.' Krystal's voice came over all thin and wimpy. Now her knees shook as much as her hands. Inside her head it felt like a big black hole had appeared that was sucking out all the pop trivia facts she'd ever known. Wow, panic!

'Stay on the line,' Ms Bored repeated, then disappeared.

'What's happening?' Carmel gabbled. 'Just stay calm, OK! You can do this! It's down to you to get us this mega-huge, big day out! No pressure, but it is!'

At last Kayleigh put a hand over Carmel's mouth to shut her up. 'Don't listen to her,' she told Krystal. 'Just take deep breaths. You'll be fine!'

'Go-go-go!' Jade urged, hopping from one foot to another.

From halfway up the stairs, Deanne beamed.

There was a long silence. Something on the phone line beeped then crackled.

Krystal swallowed hard. 'I can do this!' she told herself out loud.

'Goo-goo-grooga-ga-ga!' Kyle burbled.

'We have another caller on the line,' Melinda Swift announced to the whole world. 'It's Krystal Wilde from Hartsbridge, wanting to win this week's cool prize, which is the chance to canoodle in a canoe with Monty from Stateside.'

She paused to put on a sound-effect of water splashing and kids squealing. Then she came back on the line, her voice rising – mega-friendly, as if they'd been mates for years. 'Hey, Krystal, are you ready to play?'

Two

'Question one. Who put the "ting" in the 2001 hit, "Ting-a-ling-ling"?'

Silence. Krystal's mind was a complete blank.

Melinda chivvied her along. 'Any idea, Krystal? It was Number 1 for five weeks a couple of years back.'

'Cool Hand Luke!' The answer exploded out of nowhere. Krystal yelled it down the phone.

'Correct!' Melinda cooed. 'You had me worried for a sec there, Krystal. Now, question number two. Which band cancelled their 2003 British tour because their lead singer was in jail on assault charges?'

Woah! Krystal panicked again and glanced at Kayleigh for help.

Melinda repeated the question more slowly. 'Which band – cancelled – their 2003 British tour – because their lead singer – was in jail on assault charges? Think American here, Krystal.'

'A 2 Zee!' Kayleigh mouthed.

'A 2 Zee!' Krystal croaked.

'Cool!' Melinda accepted the answer against the background sound of a ticking clock. 'Lead singer Tommy Brooklyn faced two counts of assault after a late night bust-up outside a Los Angeles bar. A 2 Zee are now due to tour the UK later this year.'

In the Wilde family hallway, five girls grinned and crossed their fingers.

'Now, last question for Krystal Wilde out there in Hartsbridge,' mellow Melinda told the nation. 'Krystal, if you get this right, you get to ride The Extreme with Monty Del Sarto. How cool is that! You ready?'

Krystal nodded but said nothing.

'I take it that's a yes?' Melinda quipped. 'Here we go. Question number three. Which UK artist went platinum with her first single after appearing on a telly talent show?'

Tick-tick-tick. Silence from Krystal.

Kayleigh frowned. *What was that girl's name? The one with blonde hair extensions.*

Carmel pulled a face and shrugged. *Search me!*

Jade and Deanne bit their nails.

Tick-tick. Krystal's head buzzed. The single was called 'Amazing'. She had blonde hair and an eyebrow piercing. What was her name?

'We're running out of time here,' Melinda warned. 'Ooh, this is tense! We want the artist who went platinum after winning a telly talent show. C'mon, Krystal, I'm sure it's on – er – the *tip* of your tongue!'

'Lauren Tippett!' Krystal gasped.

'Co-rrect!' Melinda cried. 'Well done that gal! That's three in a row, and it wins you a family trip to Sundown. Stay on the line, Krystal, while we get groovy with a 1983 hit from smoothie smooch king, Gary Davis!'

'You did it!' Jade screeched, piling on top of a triumphant Krystal. 'That's mega!'

'Lauren Tippett!' Deanne chanted. 'D'you hear that, Buggle-mug? Krystal won!'

'And Kayleigh,' Carmel reminded everyone. 'She got the one about A 2 Zee!'

'Yeah, but it was Krystal who answered the hard ones,' Kayleigh admitted in an unusual display of generosity.

Melinda's bored assistant had come on to the phone to confirm details of the prize. 'It's happening this Saturday,' she'd informed them. 'Melinda will be there, plus Monty Del Sarto. You'll meet him and get the chance to chat with him.'

'Do we all get to go on a ride with him?' Carmel had cut in. 'There's five of us; six including the baby.'

'No babies,' the assistant had said.

'Waa-aaagh!' Kyle had wailed, as if he understood every word.

'That's why.' Ms Efficient had stuck to her guns. 'Babies can't go on the grown-up rides.'

'So five of us ride with Monty,' Krystal had persisted.

'I guess so.' The assistant had started to write down names. 'That's Krystal, and who else?'

So now Kayleigh, Krystal, Carmel, Jade and Deanne were all set for Saturday.

'Your dad will have to drive you,' Mum decided after she'd bathed Kyle and settled him into his cot. 'I'll stay home and look after Kyle.'

'Aah!' they all sighed, but inside they were glad. Kyle would only've got in the way when it came to The Wave.

'Never mind, Mum, we'll buy you a pressie!' Jade told her.

Then, when Dad came home, tired after drilling molars and buffing incisors all day, they piled on him with the good news.

'You're taking us to Sundown!' Carmel yelled. 'Y'know, the place with the pink pigs. It's gonna be cool!'

'I won it!' Krystal boasted. 'I went on national radio. I'm a star!'

'Groovy!' Dad sighed, flopping into a chair.

Krystal hugged him from behind. 'Did you hear me, Dad? I was on the radio!'

'When? What? How? Why?' he groaned, while Kayleigh handed him a drink.

So they told him.

He nodded, listened, nodded again, smoothing back his ruffled hair and escaping from his daughter's embraces. 'Nice one, Krystal. But I don't get the bit about Monty Someone. Who he?'

'Monty Del Sarto – he big star!' Kayleigh explained in a deep voice, shoving the centrefold of *Teen Dream* in front of him. 'Him date Melinda Swift. She his woman!'

The others gasped and groaned.

'No way!' Krystal said.

'Yeah, it says here,' Kayleigh insisted. In her normal voice she read out a section from the magazine. 'Hot gossip: raunchy rock star Monty Del Sarto's latest squeeze is curvaceous DJ Melinda Swift. The couple were seen in a close clinch at a recent music awards ceremony. They then posed happily for *Teen Dream*. We say: it's a match made in rock heaven!'

'Boomère!' Carmel muttered.

Kayleigh closed the mag and thought it through. 'I'm still gonna wear my new white top and denim cut-offs,' she decided.

'Yeah, and can I borrow your spray thingy?' Krystal asked her. 'I wanna do my hair like Lauren Tippett.'

Kayleigh quickly changed the subject. 'What are you gonna wear, Jade?' she asked.

'T-shirt and shorts,' came the quick reply. If you were spending the day splashing through water and fighting your way through wind tunnels you had to dress practically.

'And I think I'll wear my dinner jacket,' Dad said. 'A DJ to meet a DJ. White bow tie – the lot!'

'Don't you dare!' they cried, buffeting him with cushions. 'Anyway, you won't meet her. You're dropping us off and coming straight back home.'

Only Deanne stayed to one side, silent and thoughtful. As the others made noisy plans, she went quietly upstairs and sat on her bed.

Five tickets. She thought hard. *Only five tickets, and there were six of them. Couldn't anybody count?*

'We're all going to Sundown!' Krystal and Carmel chanted as they leaped upstairs to their own room. 'La-la-la! We're off to a theme park to meet Monty!'

'Kyle's fast asleep. Don't slam your door!' Mum called after them.

Bang! Too late.

Kayleigh, Krystal, Carmel, Jade, Deanne and Buggle-mug. Deanne counted the names on her fingers. *Yes, six!*

'You can't just wear a plain old T-shirt and shorts,' Kayleigh was telling Jade as they climbed the stairs. 'This is special. You've got to look cool.'

Six! Deanne frowned. She thought

CITY
LIBRARY
CORK

even harder. 'Listen, Buggle-mug, I know they didn't ask for a ticket for you,' she murmured. 'But that doesn't mean you're not invited.'

The invisible alien asked her how come.

'Because no one can see or hear you except me,' she explained. 'Which means there's no point getting an extra ticket, since you can just come along without anyone except the family knowing.'

Buggle-mug could see that this made sense. *Waste of a ticket*, he agreed.

'You can come on all the rides with me,' Deanne assured him. 'You'll see the giant pigs and get to meet Monty, no problem.'

Cool.

Deanne's frown lifted and she began to smile. 'It's gonna be mega!' she promised. 'I can't wait till Saturday!'

'No way!' Krystal was totally clear. 'Mum, tell Deanne that she can't bring Buggle-mug!'

'Hush, dear, you'll upset Kyle,' Mum warned.

It was Thursday teatime – the day after Krystal had won the prize. And Krystal had overheard Deanne chatting to her weird 'friend' about Saturday. 'Everyone will think we're nuts!' she claimed loudly.

'No. They'll just think Deanne is nuts,' Kayleigh pointed out. She was stretched out on the lawn, covered in sun block, sunbathing in preparation for meeting Monty.

'Oh well, that's OK then,' Krystal said. 'Not!'

Deanne's bottom lip was trembling.

'Lay off her,' Jade advised, looking up from her history homework. 'Since when did Buggle-mug do anything to you?'

'Yeah, lay off her,' Kayleigh echoed, hidden behind her sunglasses.

'We say he can't come!' For once Carmel had sided with her twin. 'Anyway, look at us; we're sitting here arguing over whether someone who doesn't even exist can come on our day out. Is that mad, or what!'

Tears appeared in Deanne's brown eyes and spilled over her lids.

'Wuuh-aaagh!' Kyle pushed out his bottom lip and wailed in sympathy.

'Now see what you've done,' Mum sighed, picking up the baby and carrying him inside.

'I've already told him he can come.' Deanne spoke up for her friend. 'No one's gonna notice him. He's promised to be really quiet.'

Jade, Carmel and Krystal stared at Deanne. Even Kayleigh took off her sunglasses and sat up. *That kid!* they all thought.

Deanne sat cross-legged on the grass, wrapped up in her own wacky world.

'He might cast a spell on you if you don't let him come!' she frowned, twisting her mouth into a tight knot. 'You'll all start talking backwards or something, then no one will be able to understand what you say!'

There was an awkward silence, while Deanne cooked up other dreadful curses.

'He won't let you come to France for the summer holiday,' she threatened. 'It'll just be him and me, Mum and Dad and Kyle playing on a beach and going swimming in the sea and eating crepes. Then you'll be sorry!'

'Boomère!' Carmel and Krystal scoffed.

'Good on you!' Jade told Deanne. 'You stick up for yourself!'

And Kayleigh smiled a grown-up smile, giving Deanne's hand a small squeeze.

'Right, let's vote!' Carmel decided. 'The question is: can Deanne bring Buggle-mug to Sundown Adventure Park, or not?'

'Yeah, like viewers ringing in to vote for popstars!' Krystal joined in with the idea. 'Or people voting off the contestant they most want to get rid of on a quiz show. Cool!'

'Yeah, vote!' Jade agreed, producing a pad of paper from her pile of home-work books. 'We have to write down our answers, yes or no!'

Deanne sat and watched in silence as Buggle-mug's fate was sealed. 'We don't care!' she muttered to him under her breath. But there was a big lump in her throat as voting began.

Kayleigh, Krystal, Carmel and Jade wrote quickly in large letters.

'OK, Jade, do you vote yes or no?' Carmel demanded.

Jade held up her crumpled piece of

paper. 'Yes!' she said loud and clear.

'Krystal, what is your vote?' Carmel prompted.

Krystal turned the paper to show her answer. 'No!' she declared.

'And my vote is No!' Carmel announced, taking her turn. 'That's two to one. Finally, Kayleigh, would you give us your vote!'

Kayleigh took a deep breath before dramatically turning her paper. 'It's "Yes!"' she said.

'Tie-break!' Carmel sighed.

'Surprise!' Kayleigh shook her head. 'Was that a waste of time, or what?'

Meanwhile, Deanne's misery went on. 'A tie-break means there's been a draw,' she explained to Buggle-mug in a hushed voice. 'We need someone to cast the deciding vote.'

Just then Mum came out of the house to call them in for supper. Carmel sprang up and raced towards her. 'Mum, you decide!' she declared.

Deanne's stomach churned. She felt hope drain away. 'That's not fair,' she protested. 'Mum's a grown-up.'

And as Mum listened and began to understand the question, Deanne saw a small cloud cross her face. She glanced in Deanne's direction, nodded at Carmel, and walked towards the jury. 'Supper's ready,' she told them, smiling at Deanne in a way that said, *This isn't what you wanted to hear, but I think it's for the best.*

Deanne uncrossed her legs and stood up. Here came the verdict, quiet but firm.

'You'd better leave Buggle-mug at home on Saturday,' Mum said. 'He can spend the day here with me and Kyle.'

Three

'Denim cut-offs and white top?' Kayleigh demanded, barging into the twins' room dressed in one of her four possible outfits for Saturday. 'Or mini-skirt and pale blue T-shirt?'

Krystal glanced up from making a sketch of the way she wanted Carmel to do her hair. 'Cut-offs,' she decided.

'Mini-skirt,' Carmel said.

Kayleigh disappeared then came back two minutes later in combats and string vest over a khaki T-shirt. 'These, or my bright pink jeans?'

Krystal showed Carmel a drawing of

long, straight hair with the front sections made into thin plaits. 'Pink jeans,' she muttered.

'Combats,' Carmel told her. 'Dream on!' she said to Krystal, shoving the sketch back across the bed.

Kayleigh sighed and twirled in front of the twins' wardrobe mirror. 'The thing is, am I gonna be hippy chick or clubby? Which d'you think Monty would prefer?'

Krystal frowned. 'Yeah, what you, Kayleigh Wilde, wear to impress the biggest name in pop is mega important!' she snorted.

Which sent thin-skinned Kayleigh nuts. 'Listen, you'd never have won this prize if it hadn't been for me!' she reminded her. 'What I wear is a big thing to me! I don't want to look like some freak, do I?'

'Me, me, me!' Krystal muttered. 'You're a fashion victim, that's what you are!'

So Kayleigh pounced on her sketch and ripped it apart. Then she broke down in tears.

'Ignore her. It's her hormones,' Carmel commented to Jade, who had just come upstairs to find out what the row was about.

'Guess what - all the kids in my class are dead jealous of us,' Jade announced. 'They want me to get Monty's autograph, and a photo of me and him on The Wave!'

She'd spent the day strutting her stuff, letting everyone know about her special trip to Sundown to meet Melinda Swift and Monty Del Sarto.

'Jade Wilde, stop telling fibs!' her teacher, Miss Adams, had scolded. She'd tapped her pen on the desk, then pointed it at Jade. 'I'm surprised at you. It's usually your sister, Deanne, who tells these weird and wonderful stories and expects us to believe them.'

'Miss, it's true!' Jade had protested.

'Miss, it is!' had come a chorus of voices. 'We all heard it on the radio!'

So Miss Adams told the staff and then the head teacher had announced it in afternoon assembly. He'd told Jade and Deanne in front of three hundred kids that he hoped the Wilde girls would behave nicely and make both the school and their family proud of them.

'Yuck!' Jade had squirmed through the final song, then sprinted for the gate before she got any more lectures.

Deanne, though, had been collared by the Big Boss. 'Have a great time,' Mr Clifford said kindly, standing in her way as she made for the door.

Deanne frowned and nodded.

'Try to look a bit happier about life, Deanne!' Miss Adams said in passing. 'It's Friday afternoon - the weekend. And tomorrow is your big day!'

The Head tilted his head sideways and studied Deanne. 'Is something wrong?'

Deanne shuffled and fidgeted. 'No.'

'Sure?' Mr Clifford took pride in showing a keen interest in all his pupils. He smiled encouragingly from behind his silver-rimmed glasses and waited for an answer.

'It's just that - well - Krystal and Carmel say - and Mum as well - that - Bug—' No, it was no good, she couldn't spit it out. Instead she went bright red and hung her head.

So Mr Clifford gave her one of his team talks. 'I think I know what's going on here,' he began. 'You're the youngest of the five Wilde girls, Deanne, and we all know from experience that your older sisters can be - well - shall we say, a little high spirited. I expect they ignore their little sister's views quite a lot of the time.'

Deanne looked up at the tall, thin figure and smiled faintly. *Yes!* she thought. *They do!*

Mr Clifford nodded. 'Well, don't let them,' he insisted. 'You stand up for yourself, Deanne. If you want to do something, then do it!'

Yes! she thought again. *I will!*

Then she went home to choose what to wear.

'No, Deanne, *not* your bridesmaid's dress!' Krystal protested.

It was pink and shiny like the Sundown pigs, and frilly, with little pearls sewn down the front. Deanne could still squeeze into it, even though it was a year since she'd worn it at their cousin's wedding. Krystal, Carmel and Kayleigh stared in horror as Deanne paraded in front of them.

'Why can't she wear it?' Jade asked. It was be-nice-to-your-kid-sister time, so that Dad could overhear and decide that she, Jade, deserved extra pocket money for the cafés and gift shops next day.

'Because!' Kayleigh, Krystal and Carmel cried.

'It's pink!' Kayleigh explained.

'And shiny,' Krystal added.

'With frills!' Carmel said.

'And not very practical,' Dad told Deanne gently. 'Why not just wear shorts and a T-shirt, like Jade?'

'No, *not* your witch's outfit!' Carmel exploded.

It was almost time for bed and Deanne was still being difficult. They were all feeling wound up and excited, and here was their kid sister parading around in a pointy hat and a black bin liner.

'I'm not going if she wears that!' Krystal declared.

You stand up for yourself! Mr Clifford had told Deanne. She frowned back at the twins.

'Don't be rotten,' Jade cut in.

Witchy-wing, witchy-woo, If you don't watch out, I'll cast a spell on yo-oou! Deanne thought.

'She's casting spells!' Krystal squealed. 'I can tell by the way she's staring at me!'

'Woo, I'm scared!' Carmel giggled. 'Deanne's gonna turn me into a frog or a spider! I'm gonna wake up in the morning with two heads!'

Kayleigh tutted. 'Grow up, you two!'

Meanwhile, Mum went upstairs and quietly laid out Deanne's clean red T-shirt and new blue shorts.

'Don't worry, Buggle-mug,' Deanne whispered in the dead of night. She'd stayed awake until the house was quiet before she'd finally let him in on her plan. Her voice sounded echoey as she crept down to the cupboard under the stairs where he slept.

'I know Krystal and Carmel have been mean,' she hissed, sitting down cross-legged on the roll of spare carpet which he used as a bed. 'But Mr Clifford says I have to stand up for myself, and I've decided that you're coming tomorrow, whatever they say!'

There was a long pause.

'Cool, huh? You'll love it. There's gonna be water rides and mega slides, and tunnels and big wheels and stuff! You can go on everything you want, Buggles – I've got free tickets. And if you're scared, you don't have to go on. You can wait without anybody noticing because you're invisible, remember. Which is cool ... And it means I can smuggle you out of the house into the car. I won't be able to talk to you much with the others around, 'cos they'll guess what I've done, but I'll make sure you're OK. I'll look after you, I promise ...'

In the airless, dark cupboard, whispering quietly, Deanne painted a secret picture of the treats to come.

They drove into Sundown Adventure Park past the pink pigs.

'Wow, they're huge!' Jade cried.

'Wicked!' Carmel gasped. Their dad had jumped the queue and told the man at the entrance who they were. They were given special plastic passes to wear around their necks, then waved straight in.

'Like we're famous!' Krystal beamed.

'Which we are, in a way,' Kayleigh assured them. She felt she knew what it would be like, waving and stepping out on to a red carpet to face a barrage of flashing cameras.

'This is it, Buggle-mug!' Deanne muttered without moving her lips.

They piled out of the car and said goodbye to Dad.

'Look after Deanne,' he reminded Kayleigh. 'And make sure Jade doesn't break anything, like an arm or a leg. We don't want her coming back home in plaster!'

'Yeah, yeah, yeah,' they all retorted. 'See ya, Dad. Bye!'

Then it was freedom, pure and simple. Time in the morning sunshine to take in the massive park with its grassy slopes and fountains, the as-yet empty gift shops and cafés, the kiddies' play-grounds, the lake in the middle, and of

course the cool grown-up rides. The Pirate Ship, The Flume, The Wave, The Corkscrew and The Extreme – they walked past each with their eyes on stalks.

'I'm starving!' Jade decided when she saw the burger bar. Her stomach rumbled and her mouth watered.

'Later!' Krystal insisted on linking up with Melinda, Monty and the other prizewinners before they did anything else. She dragged Jade away from her fries towards the entrance to the main gift shop, where they'd arranged to meet the celebs.

'What time is it?' Carmel asked, dashing ahead so that she got there before Krystal.

'Five to eleven. We're early.' Krystal wound through the thin crowd and arrived first anyway. Looking around, she found that there was no sign of the famous DJ and singer. 'Is my hair OK?' she asked Kayleigh.

'Yeah, cool.' Kayleigh was too nervous to answer properly. *Deep breaths!* she told herself. *Act like you meet Monty Del Sarto every day. Don't go all mushy!*

Carmel was already checking out the gifts in the shop window. 'Aah look, you can buy squishy pink pigs in all different sizes! Oh, and here's one made of pottery, with a slot in his head for money!'

'I'll give you a slot in your head if you don't shut up!' Krystal warned. Like Kayleigh, she was on edge about meeting the stars. 'Are you sure my hair looks OK?' she double-checked as she stared at her reflection in the shop window. Having decided against tiny plaits, she'd put it up into two bunches as usual. They were fixed in place with purple scrunchies which matched her lilac top.

'It looks normal, OK!' Carmel insisted. 'It's hair. It's brown and it grows out of your head like everyone else's.'

'You're *so* not funny,' Krystal mumbled, still tweaking anxiously at the side bits.

'When can we go on the rides?' Jade demanded, hopping from one foot to the other. She couldn't wait to get soaked through and to feel the bottom drop out of her stomach. And all for free!

'I thought you were hungry,' Kayleigh muttered. Deep breaths - in - out! She longed to see what Monty looked like in the flesh. Would his hair be natural blond or dyed? Were his eyes really that big and blue, or were they boring grey?

'Here's Melinda!' Carmel cried, losing her cool and grabbing Krystal's arm. 'Look, it is, it's her!'

And there was no doubt about it. Here was Melinda Swift - just like she looked on 'Top of the Pops' and in all the photos of her in magazines. Small and bubbly with spiky blonde hair, wearing cool make-up and a tiny skirt, with a bunch of photographers in tow. 'Hi,' she said to Jade, Krystal, Kayleigh, Carmel and Deanne. 'You must be the Wilde bunch!'

'Yeah, we're wild!' Jade yelled from the top of The Extreme. They'd met the DJ and some of the other kids who had won prizes, but not Monty, and now Jade sat in a see-through plastic pod with Kayleigh, perched at the edge of a twenty-metre drop. They were higher than a house, looking down. The pod teetered on the brink.

'I can't look!' Kayleigh jabbered. She put her hands over her eyes.

'Wheeee!' Jade cried as they dropped into space. Her stomach flipped, her knuckles went white as she gripped the front rail.

'Hee-eeelp!' Kayleigh screamed, hair flying back, mouth wide open.

They landed at the bottom with a shake, rattle and roll.

'Isn't Melinda cool?' Krystal asked Carmel. The twins were in the pod behind Kayleigh and Jade, slowly rising to the top.

'Wicked,' Carmel agreed. Her hands were sweating as they faced the extreme challenge.

'Won't it be great when Monty gets here too?' The pod hovered at the edge. It rocked forwards, ready to drop.

'Yeah, pity he's late.' Carmel prepared herself. 'The photographers seemed a bit miffed.'

Whoosh!

'Aaaagh!' the twins yelled as they plummeted.

'Magic!' Deanne's eyes sparkled. Her pod rose so high that she could see everything – the lake glittering in the sun, the long queues forming for other rides, the pink pigs by the entrance. 'They look like tiny pink mice!' she mused.

Buggle-mug sat beside her without saying a word.

'This is fun!' she insisted.

Wobble-wobble. Their plastic carriage was poised. They were on top of the world, ready for the plunge.

'Hold tight!' Deanne cried, as they fell into oblivion.

Four

'It's twelve o'clock. We've got to go back and link up with Melinda again,' Kayleigh insisted.

'Ahh, do we have to?' Carmel wanted to go on the Pirate Ship.

'Just one more ride!' Jade begged.

But big sis marched them back to the gift shop. 'Monty's gonna be there this time,' she promised. 'We have to have our photos taken.'

'If he's not there, Melinda's gonna have a major strop,' Krystal predicted as they trotted past the station for the mini steam train. The station had a proper miniature ticket office and platform, plus a full-size station master in a uniform. He waved his flag as the train choo-chooed and chugged away.

'I love that ride,' Deanne confessed quietly to Buggle-mug.

Jade gave her a sharp look and told her there was no time to stop now.

'Yeah, Melinda was already in a mood when we left her,' Carmel recalled. 'She was looking at her watch and going, "If he's still in bed I'll kill him!"'

'And all those photographers were bad-mouthing him for not showing up,' Krystal said. 'All they want is one good picture of him and Melinda and us prizewinners, then they can go home.'

'If they tell us all to smile at the camera, I'm not going to,' Jade warned. 'I hate it when they do that.' Her smile on school photos always came out gawky, with her mouth looking like a letterbox.

'I'm gonna stand next to Monty,'

Kayleigh decided. 'That's my dream – to be in a picture with him!'

'Swoon – swoon!' Carmel grinned. She spotted the knot of prizewinning kids at the gift shop entrance and dived into their midst to see what was going on.

'So where is he?' a photographer was asking Melinda. 'You said he'd be here at eleven, and it's gone twelve!'

The DJ had her back to the plate-glass window, looking less bubbly than before. 'Back off!' she pleaded to the crush of press people. There were half a dozen journalists with cameras – four men and two women, all looking angry and bored. 'Monty said he'd make it as soon as he could.'

The photographers muttered and grumbled about wanting to get home to watch the racing on TV.

'Uh-oh!' Krystal got the feeling that trouble was brewing. It was one thing Monty Del Sarto being a few minutes late, but over an hour was serious.

'Maybe he had an accident on the way here!' she whispered to Kayleigh, who went pale at the idea. Her pop hero squished in a car crash. *Oh, no!*

'Or maybe he slept in, like Melinda said,' Jade added.

Then one of the photographers spoke up. 'Look darling, just give him a tinkle, will you? Find out if he's stood you up, or what.'

Melinda glared at the man in the scruffy leather jacket. 'Monty hasn't stood me up, as you call it. He's just held up somewhere in traffic.'

'You sure?' the man challenged. He was the one who wanted to watch the 2.15 from Haydock.

Kayleigh's gaze went from one to the other, then back again.

Melinda was getting stressed out by the photographer. 'What are you trying to say?'

This time the photographer turned seriously nasty. 'Well, the last I heard, Monty Del Sarto was two-timing you with that actress from EastEnders. Maybe he's got better things to do this afternoon!'

'Where did you hear that?' Melinda gasped.

Monty – a two-timing love-rat? Never! Back and forth Kayleigh listened in horror. And by now the whole group was tuned in.

'You mean, we don't get to meet Monty after all?' one prizewinner bleated. She was a girl of about fifteen with dark hair and a bright red top. 'That was the only reason I came!'

'C'mon, where did you hear that?' Melinda blazed.

The press man shrugged. 'Everyone knows about it,' he blagged.

'Not me. This is the first I heard.'

Melinda frowned, grabbing her mobile from her bag, then turning away from the crowd to speak.

The other photographers grumbled and jostled for position to take a picture of a stroppy Melinda Swift on the phone to Monty Del Sarto. Meanwhile, the Wilde girls grouped together.

'Bummer-boomère!' Carmel complained. 'This mix-up means less time for the rides.'

'Yeah, I wanna try The Wave!' Jade agreed. 'And then the Log Flume, then the Tunnel of Fear!'

'Well, I feel sorry for Melinda,' Krystal cut in. She watched the DJ's tense face as she called her boyfriend. 'What if Monty really has dumped her?'

Kayleigh shook her head. 'He wouldn't do that. Not in public. They're a proper item – not just kissy-kissy for the cameras. I read it in my mag!'

'Ssshh!' Carmel tried to listen in to the DJ's conversation.

'Yeah, where are you now? ... You knew the arrangement ... yeah, eleven ... Don't give me that, Monty. Sure, you knew ... making me look a right idiot ... Yeah well, you'd better get here fast!'

The photographers folded their arms and chewed gum. 'So?' one said.

Melinda put her chin up and tried to look taller. 'He'll be here!' she insisted. 'Give him another half hour.'

Which meant time for one more ride before the star arrived.

'Let's try the Log Flume!' Jade cried.

Kayleigh shook her head. 'Nah, my hair will get wet.'

'Wimp!' Carmel and Krystal scoffed, making for the head of the queue.

There were shouts of 'Hey!' and 'There's a queue here, in case you hadn't noticed!'

But the girls smirked and waved their plastic passes, stepping on to a narrow log-shaped boat and sitting two by two.

'I'll kill you if my hair gets ruined,' Kayleigh mumbled, squeezing in beside Jade. Ahead lay a snaking channel of water which ran downhill between tall fake rocks. The fast-flowing stream tumbled over boulders and around bends, bubbling and churning, throwing up clouds of white spray.

'I feel sick!' Krystal wailed.

'Fasten your seat-belt,' Carmel ordered, preparing for take-off.

Meanwhile Deanne kept Buggle-mug calm. 'They're not real rapids,' she explained in a secretive whisper. 'And the log can't tip over. It's fixed to a chain under the water that pulls you along. Just sit tight and enjoy the ride.'

Krystal turned round and frowned at Deanne, but quickly turned back when she felt her stomach lurch.

They held on as the ride began, all except Jade who made a big show. 'Look, no hands!' she yelled.

The log rocked and tilted. It gathered speed towards the first bend, where the slope grew steeper and the sound of rushing water filled their ears.

'Ergh!' Krystal gulped. The log swung violently to the left, towards a boulder which it missed by a hair's breadth.

The spray rose above their heads, descending in a fine, cold shower.

'See, what did I tell you!' Kayleigh wailed through a long strand of sopping-wet hair.

Then the log surged on through the rapids, swaying and threatening to overturn. And still Jade did her 'No hands!' act, while Deanne sat calmly in the back, setting an example for her invisible friend.

Round three more bends, over a small waterfall they splashed and swished, until the fake rocks were safely negotiated and the current grew calm.

Shakily, Krystal stepped off the ride. 'I feel really sick!' she groaned. 'It's like when I was on the ferry to France last year, only worse!'

'Wicked!' was Carmel's verdict. She wrung out the hem of her shorts and squelched off in her waterlogged trainers.

Poor Kayleigh was almost in tears. 'Look at my hair! What's Monty gonna think? How am I gonna look in the photos?'

Jade gave her a hand out of the boat. 'Get over it,' she drawled.

They waited for Deanne, who seemed to be taking her time getting off the ride.

'What's she doing?' Krystal frowned, worried that Deanne was showing them up. 'Is she talking to herself, or what?'

Carmel gave one of her '*That kid!*' shrugs. 'Race you to the gift shop!'

So they ran ahead to meet the mighty Monty.

'Where is everyone?' Krystal demanded.

Their rendezvous spot was almost deserted – no Melinda, no press men, and no Monty Del Sarto! Only a boy with a thin face and a grey hoodie and baggy trousers, wearing a camera around his neck.

'They went off to the park entrance,' he announced.

Carmel gave him a dark look. 'Who are you?'

'Simon Arnley,' he said, tapping his pass. 'I won this stupid day out, didn't I? Otherwise, I wouldn't be here!'

His answer pulled Carmel up short. 'What's stupid about winning a day out at Sundown?' she quizzed.

'It's for kids,' Simon answered, looking down his nose at the window full of stuffed pigs. 'And who wants to meet some sad popstar who doesn't even show up on time?'

Carmel studied her fellow prize-winner, who was all of twelve, but whose pale face looked as though it never saw fresh air. What a waste of a prize. 'Been on any rides yet?' she challenged.

Simon curled his top lip. 'Yeah, on all of 'em,' he lied. Been there, done that. Got the T-shirt.

'So where's Monty?' Kayleigh asked, arriving after the others because she'd stopped to dry off her hair in the Ladies'.

'Some dude reckoned they saw his car in the car park,' sour-faced Simon grunted. 'So they all rushed off to form a welcoming committee for the poor guy.'

'I thought you said he was sad,' Carmel muttered.

'Yeah, he is. But no way does he deserve what Melinda's gonna do to him.' Losing interest in the whole question, Simon shoved his hands deep into his pockets and pulled out a pair of shades. 'It sucks. They don't even have a skateboard park around here,' he grumbled, hood up, head down, slouching off.

Krystal rolled her eyes, then checked her hair in the window. 'OK, race you to the pink pigs!' she announced.

A small crowd had gathered by the entrance, following every move of the photographers and the celebrity DJ.

'That's his car!' a woman insisted,

pointing to a red two-seater with the top down.

'He must be inside the park by now.' The woman's boyfriend reckoned they were all wasting their time hanging around the entrance.

'Did anyone actually see him arrive?' someone else asked, while the photographers snapped the empty sportscar.

In the shadow of the giant pigs, Carmel, Krystal, Jade, Kayleigh and Deanne sidled close to Melinda, whose mobile phone was clamped to her ear.

'I can't get a signal!' she sighed, closing her mouth in an unhappy grimace. 'God knows where he is now!'

'But that is his motor, isn't it?' the grumpy cameraman in the leather jacket asked. If not, he'd just wasted about twenty shots and his precious battery.

Melinda shook her head.

'Hold it!' the man yelled to the

scrum around the car. 'It's the wrong Ferrari, boys!'

There was a groan and lots of muttering.

'Looks like we're trying to track the Invisible Man!' someone shouted.

People nearby laughed, but Deanne grimaced. 'I'll explain why that's supposed to be funny later!' she murmured uncomfortably to Buggle-mug.

'Yeah, I'm starting to think Monty Del Sarto is the figment of someone's imagination!' Leather Jacket sneered.

Melinda blushed then tried her phone again. 'C'mon, Monty!' she pleaded, turning her back on the crowd and coming face to face with Kayleigh and company, who were backed up

against a pig's trotter. 'He said he'd be here,' she said to no one in particular. There were tears in her eyes and her bottom lip was trembling.

Kayleigh nodded. 'If he said he'd come, he'll come!'

'How weird is this!' Krystal whispered to Carmel, standing in a deep shadow, looking up at the vast underside of a pig's belly, waiting for a popstar.

'Well, sweetheart, this is where your luck runs out!' Leather Jacket announced to Melinda, loud enough for the onlookers to hear. 'You might have got your mugshot with Monty on the front pages once upon a time, but that was last week!'

The DJ shook her head. Her bubbly manner had drained away, her face was pale and strained.

'Yeah.' The press pack was breaking up in disgust. 'If you ask me, he never was coming. She got us here under false pretences!'

'Don't listen!' Krystal told Melinda. 'Monty won't let you down!'

But the DJ glanced over her shoulder at the angry journalists and a disappointed crowd. 'This will be in all the gossip columns. Word will get around – DJ lures kids to theme park with false promise. My radio bosses are gonna kill me!'

Gradually the idea that Monty might not make it sank in. No mega meeting with the lead singer from Stateside. What a let down! Jade turned to Carmel with a frown, Deanne looked worried. Even Kayleigh and Krystal felt less sure than they'd sounded a minute earlier.

And to make matters worse, the man in the leather jacket wanted the last word.

'Monty's moved on!' he told Melinda with a cruel smile. 'Face it, darling – you're well and truly dumped!'

Five

Click-click-click. The photographers took cruel photos of Melinda Swift in tears.

'I suppose it's better than nothing,' one muttered.

'Yeah – "Top DJ Toppled by Rival in Love-Scrap!"'

'Don't you just hate them?' Kayleigh murmured to Krystal. She'd got used to the idea of a no-show from Monty and was starting to feel really sorry for Melinda.

Krystal nodded. 'I hope ... I hope their lenses crack!'

As the photographers took their

pictures then drifted away, Deanne grabbed the chance to chat to Bugglemug, taking him to one side and talking in a low voice. 'The thing is, I know you didn't like that joke about the Invisible Man,' she began. 'Neither did I. But some people don't care about hurting other people's feelings, and that man in the leather jacket wasn't very nice ...'

Back under the biggest pink pig, Melinda smudged her make-up as she wiped her eyes with the back of her hand. 'Right,' she said, 'if Monty Del Sarto reckons he can dump me just like that, I say he's not worth my time. He can ... go take a running jump!'

Kayleigh and Krystal were shocked by the sudden turnaround. 'I thought you two were in love!' Kayleigh gasped.

'Were!' Melinda frowned. 'That's the past tense. Not any more.'

'You mean, Monty's history?' Krystal rode the Big Dipper of Melinda's emotions – up-down-up.

The DJ nodded. 'Definitely. The guy can't even show up like he promised. Oh sure, he says the right things when we're together; like he loves me and all that stuff. But what does it mean when it comes to action? A big round zero, that's what!'

Kayleigh couldn't believe what she was hearing about her pop hero. 'Maybe there's been some mistake,' she suggested.

Melinda ran a hand through her hair. 'Yeah, *my* mistake – to trust him in the first place!' She dug in her pocket for her car keys. 'I'm sorry your day has been such a wipe-out,' she told the girls. 'Tell the others I'm out of here!'

'... the Invisible Man was in a film on TV.' Deanne struggled on with her explanation. 'I think he was normal, then he was zapped by some rays from a ray-gun and he turned invisible. Then he had to wear bandages round his face ...' She paused to check on Kayleigh and the others, noticed Melinda storming off towards the car park, then turned back. '... Buggle-mug?'

There was no answer.

'Buggle-mug!' Deanne said a second time. 'Where are you?'

The silence went on.

'Don't mess around,' Deanne pleaded, beginning to search frantically on the grassy slope. She ran between pigs' legs, under the big sign saying 'Sundown Adventure Park'. But there was no sign of her alien.

'Everything's gone pear-shaped!' Carmel complained.

Melinda Swift had stormed off in a strop over Monty Del Sarto and left all the prizewinners grumbling.

'Don't blame us!' Jade protested to the fifteen-year-old girl in the red top after she'd delivered the bad news. 'It's not our fault that Monty's dumped Melinda!'

'Sshhh!' Kayleigh warned. But it was too late. The rumour started by the photographer took hold and spread like wildfire around the park.

'What do we do now?' Krystal asked, once she'd dragged Deanne back into the group.

'B-b-but!' Deanne had protested, waving her arm wildly towards the hill with the pigs.

'What's up?' Jade asked.

Deanne bit her lip and shook her head.

'Well c'mon then, let's go back and ride The Wave!' Jade suggested. 'We're not gonna let the Melinda and Monty thing spoil our day!'

Sighing and mumbling, the others agreed.

'C'mon, Deanne!' Carmel insisted, tugging her by the hand.

Deanne gave in, though her head was in a spin. *Buggle-mug had vanished! One minute he was there, the next he was gone. But how could she tell anyone, when he wasn't meant to be here in the first place? And since only she could see him, how could she ask the others to help her look for him? Poor Buggle-mug, all alone and lost!*

'We'll do The Wave first, then The Corkscrew.' Jade lined up the best rides - the ones that threw you about, turned you upside down, soaked you to the skin and generally terrified you. She set off at a trot to make up for lost time, skipping the queue and nipping into the first available boat. 'There's room for all five of us,' she declared.

Kayleigh, Krystal, Carmel, Jade and Deanne climbed in after her, feeling the slight rock of the small yellow boat as they settled into the seats.

'We must be mad!' Kayleigh mumbled, looking out across a rough pond where a machine made waves that rose and fell.

Once again, Krystal felt her stomach churn. 'Yeah, totally mad!' she grumbled.

'Wicked!' Carmel cried as they set off.

Ahead of them, a wave rose. The boat bobbed, crested the wave and dropped down the far side. This happened three times – up and down through the choppy water.

'Cool!' Jade grinned, glancing down at her splashed T-shirt. 'Now for the big one!'

This time a glittering wall of water rose before their eyes. Slowly the boat rose up and up.

Kayleigh gritted her teeth, preparing for the huge wave to break. She looked down to check how high they were, saw people in the crowd looking up at them, including a man standing under a tree in a baseball cap and dark glasses. Her heart skipped a beat. 'Monty!' she cried.

'Aaaagh!' Krystal and Carmel screamed.

The wave towered over them, tilting their boat almost vertical. It curled and broke, the boat powered its way through the white spray and bobbed down the far side.

'How cool was that!' Jade yelled to her drowned-rat sisters.

'Cool!' Krystal and Carmel agreed, now that it was over.

'M-M-Monty!' Kayleigh gasped.

The boat bobbed and rocked to a standstill by a jetty. 'What?' Krystal asked Kayleigh with a frown.

'Monty – I saw him – under a tree –

back there!' Kayleigh could hardly get her words out.

'You mean, Monty Del Sarto? *The* Monty!' Krystal shook her head.

Carmel laughed. 'No way!'

'I did, honest! In sunglasses. It was definitely him!' Without waiting for the others, Kayleigh sprang out of the small boat and sprinted off.

She ran by the side of the wave machine, ignoring the squeals of the people in the next boat, until she came to the tree where Monty had been standing.

'Yeah, where is he, then?' Jade screeched to a halt beside Kayleigh.

Nothing. No one. Only a litter bin stuffed full of empty ice cream tubs. 'He must have moved!' Kayleigh claimed.

'So?' Carmel and Krystal demanded.

Deanne darted under the tree, looked behind the trunk and the bin, but came back empty-handed.

'He was here,' Kayleigh told them. 'He's wearing a baseball cap and shades ...'

'Like a zillion other people!' Carmel snorted. 'Honestly, Kayleigh, you don't expect us to believe–'

'There he is!' Kayleigh pointed at a figure walking towards the gift shop and cafés. He was tall, dressed in a denim jacket and khaki combats, a fawn cap covering his short blond hair.

Jade frowned at the man's back view. 'That's not him!' she scoffed.

''Tis!'

''Tisn't!'

'I'm telling you, it is!' Once more Kayleigh sprinted off, with the others close behind.

They followed the suspect to the doors of the busy gift shop, then hid behind a corner while he tried to use his mobile phone.

'See!' Kayleigh insisted.

Krystal took a closer look. 'It could be Monty,' she whispered.

'No way!' Jade still refused to believe it. 'What would a mega pop star be doing wandering around on his own?'

'He's keeping low key, looking for Melinda, stupid!' Kayleigh had it all worked out. 'He's late, so he's guessing that she's already left, and now he's trying to call her, but she's turned her phone off 'cos she's mad with him, and now he doesn't know what to do!'

'Hmmm.' Carmel studied the figure in the cap, then went to fetch Deanne from behind an ice cream kiosk. 'What's wrong with you?' she demanded.

'Nothing!' Deanne sighed. *Bugglemug, come back, please!*

The hissing and whispering went on.

''Tis!'

''Tisn't!'

''Tis!'

'Oh, puh-lease!' Carmel broke in. She stood clear of the corner and marched straight up to the man in the shades. 'Are you Monty Del Sarto from

Stateside?' she asked in a clear voice.

He coughed and shook his head. 'No, sorry.'

Carmel thought the cough was suspicious. 'Sure?' she double-checked. 'My sister, Kayleigh, says you're him.'

From behind the wall, Kayleigh groaned.

'Well, I'm not,' the man snapped, turning and walking away towards a fountain in the middle of a courtyard.

Aha – another shady move! Carmel beckoned the others to join her. 'I think it's him!' she gasped.

Kayleigh nodded, her eyes sparkling with excitement. 'He finally came!'

It was Jade who pulled them back down to earth. 'Am I deaf, or did he just deny it?' she asked.

'That's because he doesn't want fans mobbing him while he's looking for Melinda,' Krystal pointed out. 'Go on, Kayleigh, you go and talk to him!'

So Kayleigh took a deep breath and marched up to their pop star, planning what she would say. She gazed up into the tanned, handsome face. 'If you want to know what happened to Melinda, we can tell you,' she said simply.

And that was it. Monty Del Sarto took off his dark glasses and stared down at Kayleigh. His eyes, she was happy to report later, were as big and blue as they appeared in the centrefold of *Teen Dream*.

Monty took the excited girls into a café and sat them down at a corner table overlooking the lake.

'This is all my fault,' he admitted. 'I had the time to meet in my diary as one o'clock, not eleven.'

'Melinda was mad with you,' Krystal

warned. 'The photographers gave her a hard time and then she stormed off.'

Monty shrugged. 'She knows what I'm like about being on time. I always get it wrong.'

'But that wasn't the main reason,' Carmel explained. She didn't bother with any fancy words, she just went straight to the point. 'She's mad because you dumped her for the woman in EastEnders.'

Ms Tactful! Kayleigh and Krystal covered their eyes and held their breath.

Monty sat back on two legs of his chair. 'Dumped? What woman in EastEnders?' It was the first he'd heard of it.

Kayleigh felt it was down to her to soften the story and save Monty's feelings. 'It's just some stupid rumour,' she explained. 'I knew you wouldn't cheat on Melinda like that.'

'I wouldn't. I didn't!' Monty insisted,

a troubled look appearing in his cornflower-blue eyes.

'But people believe everything they hear. Before you knew it, they were taking pictures of her crying ...'

'Crying?' Monty echoed, looking really worried now. 'Wow, that doesn't sound good. What did she say?'

Kayleigh cleared her throat, trying to think of a nice way to put this next bit.

'She said you were history,' Carmel stepped in and told him bluntly. 'She said she made a big mistake to trust you in the first place.'

Monty's face went pale. 'That bad, huh?'

'But you can ring her.' To Carmel it seemed easy-peasy. 'Get on the phone and explain.'

To their surprise, Monty refused. 'No. If she believes stuff like that without even checking with me first, then let her sweat a bit,' he decided. 'Listen, I'm not saying I don't really like Mel, 'cos I do. She's my kind of girl – y'know, she's genuine, not plastic and into all that celeb stuff like most people I meet.'

'Well then?' Carmel still didn't get it.

'But she has to trust me. OK, so I was late. But no way did I make a move on the EastEnders chick. So now I'm mad because she's mad!'

Jade glanced at Carmel. Wow, was this complicated.

'But if you don't call her, how can you two make up?' Kayleigh asked. She could see a disaster opening up before her eyes.

Monty drained his coffee cup and shrugged. 'Maybe this is the end,' he muttered gloomily. 'Maybe I'm through with Melinda after all. Yeah, that's it, it's over.'

Six

Carmel and Jade followed Deanne into the Ladies'. They found her sobbing by the sinks.

'Hey, it's not that bad!' Jade exclaimed. 'People break up all the time. And we hardly even know Monty and Melinda, except what we read about them in Kayleigh's mags. What's to cry about?'

Deanne sniffed and snivelled. 'It's not that,' she mumbled.

She'd got up from the table and stumbled off as Monty had declared that he was through with Melinda.

Kayleigh had sat in shocked silence. Krystal had tried to put things another, softer way. 'Maybe Melinda was too upset to think straight,' she'd pointed out. 'When she said you were history, maybe she didn't really mean it.'

But Kayleigh had given her a warning dig in the ribs. Monty was still mad, and not listening to reason. 'Can I have your autograph, please?' she'd asked, briskly changing the subject and thrusting a notepad under his nose. 'I really like your music – it's cool!'

'Me too!' Krystal had chimed in, her eyes wide with adoration. 'It was me who won the competition!'

So Monty had come round to signing autographs and Carmel and Jade had chased after Deanne.

'If you're not crying over Monty and Mel, what are you blubbing about?' Jade asked.

Deanne sniffed loudly. 'Nothing.'

'Is it 'cos you won't get your pic

in the paper?' Carmel asked.

'No.'

'I know! It's 'cos Krystal and Kayleigh were mean and said Buggle-mug couldn't come!' Jade guessed.

'Uhhh!' Deanne sobbed, burying her face in a paper towel. 'But ... smuggled ... no one noticed ... on the rides!'

'Slow down,' Carmel coaxed. 'Did I hear that right? You brought Buggle-mug anyway and smuggled him on to the rides?'

'Yep!' Deanne hiccoughed.

'Wicked!' Jade laughed. 'So what's to cry about? Did he fall off The Extreme when no one was looking?'

Deanne's sobs grew louder. 'Worse,' she admitted. 'He ran off by the pink pigs and got lost!'

Once Monty had started signing autographs, there was no stopping.

'Hey, it's Monty Del Sarto!' the girl with the red top squeaked from across the café. 'He showed up after all. Wow, Monty! Can you sign this?'

She led a bunch of prizewinners in a queue that quickly reached the café door and snaked out into the courtyard. Even Simon, the kid in the grey hoodie, queued up with a camera for a picture of the popstar.

'Sorry about that!' Kayleigh said to Monty as he sat and signed.

Click! Simon started snapping from a few metres back.

'Yeah, you blew my cover,' he agreed, but she could tell he wasn't annoyed. 'I was hoping no one would recognize me.'

Scribble-scribble - he was Mr Nice Guy, scrawling his name on slips of paper, official passes, even T-shirts.

'You're the best, Monty!' fans sighed. 'We love you!'

Click! Click! Simon snapped the happy mob.

Bleep-bleep, bleep-bleep. Monty's phone rang from inside his jacket pocket, but he was too busy to answer it. He looked up at Krystal and Kayleigh. 'Get me out of here!' he mouthed.

Kayleigh thought and acted fast. 'Time to take us on a ride!' she announced. 'Y'know, as part of our prize!'

Monty stared down the queue. 'All of you?' he panicked.

Kayleigh nodded. 'Yeah, we can all fit on the train through the Tunnel of Fear. Krystal and me will sit in the first carriage with you.'

'You will?' Still unsure, Monty slowly got to his feet. 'After that, can I go home?'

'Yeah, we'll definitely let you after you've been on the ride,' Krystal promised. 'All you have to do is sit on the train!'

Before he could say no, Kayleigh grabbed his jacket from the back of his chair. 'Let's get this over with,' she suggested. 'The exit from the Tunnel of Fear is near the main gate, so you can hop off and sneak straight out!'

She and Krystal led the way out of the café.

'Once you're out of here, you can call Melinda and make up,' Krystal told Monty with a hopeful smile. 'Tell her you're sorry.'

But he frowned and shook his head. 'No, it's down to her this time,' he insisted, carried along by the crowd past the gift shop, out into the park.

Krystal and Kayleigh sighed. Celebs were stubborn, they realized. They needed more help than most people to kiss and make up.

'OK, we'll look for him together,' Jade promised. 'We'll seek him here, we'll seek him there – we'll seek that alien everywhere!' She mopped Deanne's tears with a fresh towel. 'Did you hear me? I said, we'll start a big search for Buggle-mug.'

'Th-th-thanks!' Deanne gulped.

Carmel led the way out of the loos into the courtyard, just in time to see Kayleigh and Krystal leading Monty and a bunch of excited fans towards the Tunnel of Fear. 'How exactly are we gonna do this?' she demanded. 'Do we run around asking if people have seen an invisible alien, or what?'

'Hmmm.' Jade's plan hadn't led her this far. In fact, her main idea was to try out as many different rides as possible while faking the search. 'What kind of noise does Buggles make, Deanne? Does he speak English?'

Their little sister shook her head. 'He just sort of thinks, and I can understand him.'

'Great!' Carmel sighed. 'We can't see him, we can't hear him. This is mad!'

'Take no notice!' Jade said firmly, sprinting into the sunshine. 'Let's try the Pirate Ship first. C'mon, Deanne, sit in

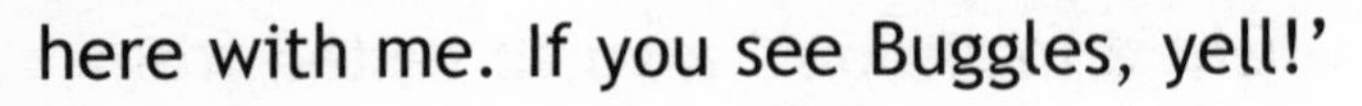

here with me. If you see Buggles, yell!'

'I'm not sure about this Tunnel of Fear thing,' Monty confessed.

Kayleigh and Krystal paused beside an ornamental fountain, under a giant sign that said, 'Be Afraid. Be Very Afraid!'

'It's OK,' Kayleigh assured him. 'It's just voices and ghosts swooshing out in front of you in the dark.'

'Your worst fears are about to come true!' another sign said.

The crowd shoved Monty forward to the gloomy entrance, where a creature, half man, half wolf, snarled from behind iron bars.

'I'll wait here!' Krystal suddenly volunteered, nervously clutching the celeb's denim jacket to her chest.

'Wimp!' Kayleigh sneered.

Krystal flashed her a hard look. 'I mean, I'll wait to see that everyone gets on,' she lied. 'And I'll look after Monty's jacket.'

'Get a move on!' a voice called from behind. People shoved, the queue edged forward.

Still Kayleigh looked over her shoulder at Krystal. 'How come you don't want to ride?' she hissed.

Click! Simon snapped the werewolf behind the bars.

'Live your Nightmares!' a hollow voice whispered.

'How come?' Kayleigh whispered again.

'Just go!' Krystal urged.

The wolf-man howled, the first carriage clattered along the rails into the tunnel and darkness swallowed Monty and Kayleigh.

*

This is gonna be very cool! Krystal promised herself. She knew her scared act hadn't fooled Kayleigh, but it had worked well enough to leave her free to carry out a major mission!

Aim of mission – to get Melinda and Monty back together.

Reason – because M and M were too proud to say sorry.

Method – involving the use of Monty's phone.

Time allowed – five minutes.

Quickly Krystal dipped into the popstar's jacket pocket and drew out his mobile phone.

Creak-groan-creak! Inside the Tunnel of Fear, doors swung open and clattered shut. Hairy spiders swung down from the roof, rats scuttled along dripping gutters.

'Ooh-aagh!'

'Eek!'

'What was that?'

Kayleigh sat calmly in the front carriage. Spiders didn't spook her, and she knew the rats weren't real.

In the background, the sound of a human heartbeat grew louder – *buh-boom, buh-boom!* Then witchlike hands clutched at passengers' hair while giant moths fluttered against flickering lights.

'Isn't this cool?' Kayleigh asked Monty.

He sat rigid in his seat, hands clenched. 'Moths aren't really my thing,' he confessed.

'You are entering the flaming abyss!' a voice moaned from the darkness.

Suddenly the carriage seemed to plummet down a narrow chasm. A hot wind blew against their cheeks, there were flames below.

'Aaagh!' Monty gulped, grabbing Kayleigh by the hand. He kept hold when the carriage levelled out and the flames disappeared.

'That was a fake fire,' Kayleigh assured him.

Monty glanced nervously in every direction. 'How much longer?' he whispered.

'Only a couple of minutes.' Kayleigh looked down at the popstar's hand tightly clasping hers and grinned to herself. 'The next bit is quite scary though.'

Back and forth the Pirate Ship swung, high above the crowds.

'Avast, mi hearties!' Jade cried.

'Not so loud. People are staring,' Carmel complained. 'What's that mean, anyway?'

Jade shaded her eyes with one hand and looked far out to sea. 'Dunno. It's what pirates say. Watch out, you land-lubbers! We're coming to plunder your treasure, ooh-aah!'

Carmel sat back with Deanne in the giant swing. 'Any sign of Buggle-mug yet?' she asked, just to show willing.

'No, nothing. You will help me look, won't you?'

In spite of herself, Carmel agreed. 'He can't have gone far,' she soothed. 'Anyway, he's gonna be hungry soon, then he'll come and find you.'

Deanne nodded more hopefully. 'I've got a secret signal,' she admitted. 'If I make my eyes go crossed, like this, it means he has to come.'

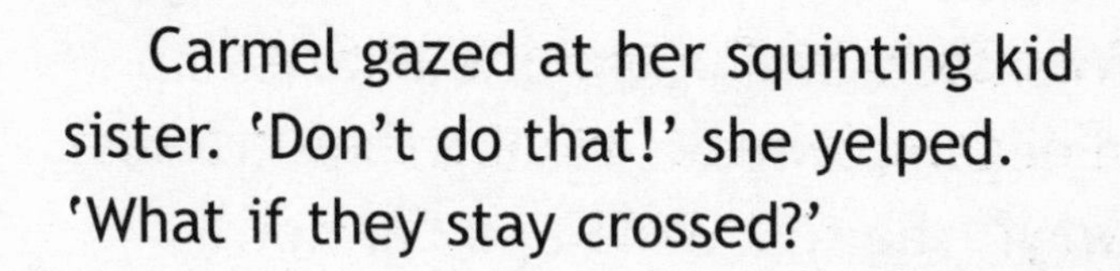

Carmel gazed at her squinting kid sister. 'Don't do that!' she yelped. 'What if they stay crossed?'

'Yeah, something like that would really work!' Jade commented sarcastically. 'This thought exchange stuff ... tele-graphy, tele-visionary, tel-something?'

'Telepathy,' Carmel told her with a smug smile.

By now the Pirate Ship was slowing and steadying after three wild minutes on a stormy sea. 'Time to walk the plank, mi hearties!' she crowed.

Deanne stood up on wobbly sea legs. 'No, wait!' she cried, pointing across the theme park towards the exit and the pink pigs beyond. 'There he is! He's waiting where I last saw him!'

'What a sensible little alien!' Carmel said with a sigh of relief. 'Telepath him. Tell him to stay there until we come and fetch him,' she told Deanne.

'Can't. He's too far away.' Quickly she jumped down from the Pirate Ship and began to weave through the crowds. 'Hurry!' she told Jade and Carmel.

'Tutt!' Jade grumbled. *The things they did for that kid!*

Soon the pigs loomed overhead, their round bellies casting long shadows over the grassy hill, daisies and buttercups sprinkling the ground by their feet.

'OK, so where is this precious friend?' Carmel demanded. 'We're wasting time here, and I'm losing my temper!'

'Gone!' Deanne cried. 'He didn't wait for us!'

Jade and Carmel filled the air with groans, until Carmel saw something that took her mind totally off the missing Buggle-mug. 'Hey, isn't that Melinda in the black car?'

Jade looked, and yes, the DJ was cruising round the car park looking for a space.

They ran up to her and flagged her down. 'We thought you'd gone!' they cried.

Melinda's eyes were red and puffy, her spiky hair lay flat against her head.

'I felt bad about storming off,' she told them. 'Run and tell the other prizewinners that I'm finding a place to park.'

Krystal pressed 'Unlock' on Monty's phone. Then 'Phone Book'. Then she ran through all the names. Andy, Charlotte, Chris, Dad ... Karli, Mel 1, Mel 2, Mum ... Rapidly she tapped back up the list. *Mel 1, Mel 2. OK, so which one is Melinda?*

Time was slipping by. She had to make a decision.

Maybe they're both Melinda! she thought. *One for her home number, and one for her mobile. Yeah, that was it!* Eenie-meenie, minie-mo - which one should she text?

Both! What harm was there in that? Yeah, both of Mel's numbers.

After all, the message was simple, and it was guaranteed to make Melinda come running back into Monty's arms.

Carefully Krystal tapped in the message. "I luv u – Monty!!" She read it back, then sent it to Mel 1.

Then she did the whole thing over again for Mel 2. "I luv u – Monty!!"

Smiling, she was about to slip the phone back into Monty's pocket when it rang. On the little screen the number showed that it was a call from Mel 1.

'Wow, that didn't take long!' Krystal said out loud. Her text message had worked like a dream. Melinda was on the phone ready to make up the lovers' tiff. Magic!

But now, to answer it, or not to answer it – that was the question!

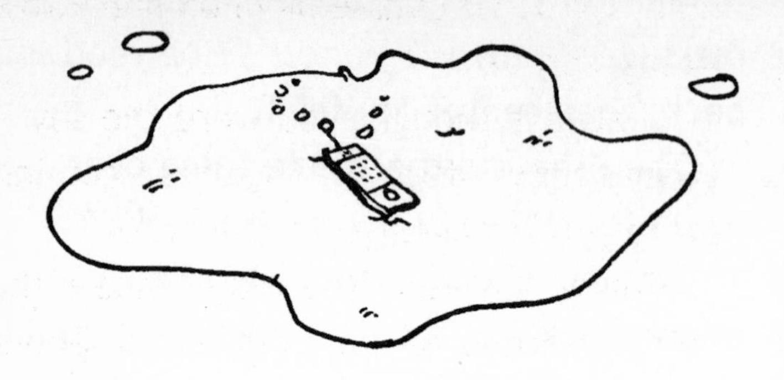

Seven

Yeah – take the call!

Krystal made up her mind in a flash. Monty himself was emerging from the Tunnel of Fear. All she, Krystal, had to do was blag her way through a conversation with Melinda for thirty seconds until the popstar got out of the carriage.

She pressed the key, ready to take the call.

'Oh Monty!' a woman's voice gushed. 'Your message is so cute! I didn't know you cared!'

Krystal frowned. This didn't sound

quite right. Of course Melinda knew that Monty cared!

'I always thought you were the shy type, Monty. After all, I've been coming on to you for ages.'

Funny, it wasn't the right voice either – Krystal frowned and pressed the phone closer against her ear.

'And when we last met at that award ceremony, I seem to recall there was a little blonde thing hanging on your arm – some girl DJ. I still came on pretty strong, gave you my mobile number and everything, without getting very far. But now I receive a full-on smoochy message – wow!'

Ergh! Krystal almost dropped the phone in shock. She stumbled back against the low wall surrounding the fountain and sat down with a jolt.

'Hey, Monty, say something,' the voice went on. 'Don't pretend you don't know who this is – it's Mel. Melanie Beeston from EastEnders!'

'Hi, Krystal!' Kayleigh yelled. 'Give Monty his jacket. He has to leave!'

Monty staggered out of the carriage after Kayleigh – white as a sheet, with trembling limbs.

Krystal panicked. Melinda wasn't Melinda. Oh no, bummer, bummer, boomère! She put on her deepest voice and spoke into the phone. 'Mel, you got the wrong idea there, babe.'

There was a pause. 'Monty?' Melanie quizzed.

'Yeah. Erm, listen. I didn't send any message, OK!'

'What's wrong with your voice?' the actress said. 'Anyway, don't be stupid. 'Course you sent me a message. I just read it. It came from your mobile number, so don't give me that garbage.'

'Erm – er!' Krystal was stuck. 'Listen, I don't love you!' she said gruffly. Better give it to her straight.

Melanie grew madder. 'Is this a wind-up, or what?'

Meanwhile, Kayleigh dragged a shaky Monty towards the fountain. 'C'mon, Krystal, he has to make a quick getaway. What're you doing with that phone?'

'Yeah!' Monty added in a confused voice. 'That looks like my mobile from here!'

'Monty? Stop messing around.' Melanie lowered her voice to a sexy whisper. 'There's no need to be shy. Do you want to meet me for a drink, or would you rather I came round to your place?'

'No!' Krystal squeaked. Kayleigh and Monty were five metres away, demanding explanations. What now? She looked this way and that, saw the rest of the prizewinners tumbling out of the Tunnel, saw Carmel, Jade and Deanne trotting towards the fountain from another direction – and suddenly it was all too much. 'Whoops!' she cried, accidentally on purpose squeezing Monty's mobile between her hands as if it was a slippery bar of soap.

The phone shot up in the air, curved back down, and - *plop* - landed in the fountain.

Gurgle-gurgle-ssss-bleep!

'You dummy!' Kayleigh told Krystal, at least fifty times.

'S-s-sorry!' Krystal gasped. She lay flat on the low wall and fished for the phone.

'Hey, Ms Butterfingers,' Monty said, helplessly standing by as his fans caught up with him again. 'What happened?'

I cut Melanie Beeston off in the nick of time – that's what happened! Krystal thought. Her fingers trawled the bottom of the pool, dredged up two ice cream cartons and a twenty pence piece. *Phew, that was close!*

'The phone's gonna be ruined anyway!' Kayleigh went on.

Krystal fished again and found it. She drew it up from the sludgy bottom and presented Monty with it. 'S-sorry!'

she stammered yet again.

It was Kayleigh who was the maddest. 'Don't you know you shouldn't use someone's phone without asking!' she yelled. 'That's private property. Monty trusted you to look after it!'

'Monty!' His fans, led by Red-Top, were upon him. 'Sing something for us. Tell us a joke. When's your next live concert? Monty, you're cool!'

Simon the Snapper kept on taking pics of the international star being mobbed.

Krystal wiped her dripping arms and hands on her skirt. 'It was ringing. I was just answering it,' she explained. *Well, it was half-true!*

'It's dead,' Monty shrugged. 'Man, I feel like I just lost a part of myself – that phone had all my main numbers in it!'

'Monty, can we take some more pictures?' his fans clamoured. The crowd grew bigger and cut off his exit route to the car park.

He was centre of attention once more.

'Poor guy!' Kayleigh muttered, throwing Krystal an angry look.

Krystal drew a deep breath and took Kayleigh to one side. 'It's worse than you think,' she confessed. The knowledge of what she'd just done was lying in the pit of her stomach like a lumpy stone. She had to tell someone, and that someone was her already angry big sister.

Kayleigh narrowed her eyes. 'What do you mean, *worse*?'

'I was trying to help,' Krystal squirmed.

'But?'

'But – I didn't.'

Kayleigh gave an exasperated sigh. 'Come on, spit it out. What did you do?'

Another deep breath, and then it came pouring out. 'Texted – Mel 1 and Mel 2 – that TV actress – honest! – I used Monty's voice – she invited herself to his place!' There, she'd said it! Now she felt hollow, stupid and really sorry.

'Stop!' Kayleigh groaned. 'Don't tell me any more. This is a total nightmare!' She glanced at poor Monty and wondered exactly how they were going to explain this one.

'Give me a break,' he was pleading to his fans. 'I need to go now.'

'No way!' they yelled. 'Sign this! We love you, Monty!'

Red-Top was turning out to be his number one fan. 'Tell us the rumour isn't true!' she begged, grabbing his hand in front of the whole crowd.

'What rumour?' he asked, looking over the top of the crowd for help from Kayleigh. The look said, *Get me out of here!*

'The one about you and that soapstar, Melanie Thingy. They're saying that you two are an item.'

'Uh-oh!' Krystal moaned, hiding her face behind her hands while Monty tried to deny the rumour.

'Krystal, Krystal!' Carmel called. She balanced on the wall of the fountain at the far side from the scrum of fans.

'Not now,' Kayleigh warned. 'We're busy.'

'No, listen!' Jade had jumped up beside Carmel and was waving madly. 'What's Monty still doing here?'

'He can't get away, can he?' Kayleigh yelped. 'He got cornered, and it's all Krystal's fault.'

Jade and Carmel balanced like tightrope walkers around the fountain, arms spread wide, stepping gingerly. 'C'mon, Deanne!' they encouraged.

'Mel Beeston and I are not seeing each other,' Monty said firmly. 'That's

N-O-T, not! No way. Never have been. Never will be, period!'

Serious Simon scribbled down Monty's words on the palm of his hand.

Wobble-wobble – Jade finally reached Krystal and Kayleigh. 'Bad news!'

'Not more!' Kayleigh shook her head as if she couldn't take it. 'Is it to do with Buggle-mug? Did you find him?'

'Nope and nope,' Jade said.

Deanne balanced behind her sisters, bottom lip trembling.

'What then?'

Carmel beckoned Kayleigh and Krystal. 'We just saw Melinda!'

'Where?'

'When?'

'In the car park,' Jade told them. 'She came back 'cos she didn't want to let the prizewinners down. I suppose she thinks the split with Monty ruined our day, which shows how cool she is, because she wants to make it up to us.'

Kayleigh swallowed hard. 'Yeah, she's

OK. But does she know that Monty finally showed up?'

'Nope,' Jade answered. 'She's parking, then she's coming to find us.'

'Is she still mad with him?' Krystal asked. It looked like they were faced with a humungous problem.

'More upset than mad,' Carmel judged, remembering Melinda's red eyes and splotchy face. 'I just know it wouldn't be good for them to meet up right now.'

'Right!' Kayleigh and Krystal agreed.

They all looked at Monty mobbed by fans, then in the direction of the pink pigs, looming on the skyline.

In a couple of minutes at the most, Melinda would be walking this way. She would see Monty being adored. She would lay into him with, 'You cheated on me!'

'No, I didn't!'

'Yes, you did!'

In public, with everyone staring.

Krystal closed her eyes. 'What do we do now?' she groaned.

Eight

'The tabloid newspapers suck,' Monty said to his fans. 'A couple of months back they had me practically hitched to a Hollywood babe who I hadn't even met!'

'Oh, why can't they leave him alone?' Kayleigh sighed. 'The poor guy's going through a personal trauma. When you're having a major row with your girlfriend you need your own space!'

Jade grimaced. 'What's a trauma?' she muttered. 'Is it a new ride, or what?'

'You can't see it, stupid!' Carmel hissed. 'It's just something you go through – a crisis.'

'Whatever.' From the low wall she could see above the heads of Monty and his fans. 'I'm keeping a lookout for Melinda ... Uh-oh, here she comes now!'

In the distance Jade made out the slight blonde figure of the DJ walking quickly in their direction.

'Eek!' Carmel squeaked. She turned to Deanne. 'Do something!'

Deanne turned her thoughtful brown eyes on Monty. She seemed to reach a decision, then she shoved through the crowd to reach him.

'Hey,' Monty murmured to her when she tugged at his hand. He stopped signing autographs and looked down. 'What's the problem?'

'I'm Deanne Wilde,' she reminded him. 'I'm seven and a half.'

He stooped to listen. 'Yeah, I remember. You don't look like you're having a good time. Why not?'

Deanne let the tears well up. 'I lost my friend,' she explained. 'He's called Buggles. I looked everywhere.'

Monty frowned. 'I don't remember seeing him. How old is – er – Buggles?'

'The same age as me. He's not from around here. He'll be lost and scared.'

'Melinda's coming!' Jade warned a second time. The radio star had spotted the crowd and was advancing with a grim look in her eye. Still, Jade couldn't be sure whether Melinda had seen Monty.

Krystal dived into the mob and grabbed the pop star. 'Follow me!' she hissed.

But Monty pulled back. 'Hold it. I'm talking to Deanne here. She has a serious problem. Where did you last see your friend?' he asked.

Deanne sniffed and spoke up. 'By the pigs. Jade and Carmel and me nearly found him there, then we lost him again. Will you help us look?'

Watching from a little way back in the crowd, Kayleigh marvelled at how Deanne could worm her way into a person's good books. With just one long look, Monty was melting before their eyes.

'Yeah, sure I'll help,' he agreed, letting himself be led by the hand. 'Where to now?'

Deanne broke through the fans on the side of the crowd furthest from Melinda. She scanned the theme park, with its death-defying rides, dodgems and carousels. 'The mini-train!' she announced. 'We haven't searched there so far!'

'Melinda!' The girl in the red top and Snapper Simon led the charge towards the DJ, giving Monty, Deanne, Krystal and Kayleigh the chance to sneak away.

Melinda stopped and raised both hands. 'Woah!'

'C'mon!' Jade cried to Carmel, leaping down from the fountain and outsprinting everyone. She screeched to a halt at Melinda's side. 'They've gone nuts!' she gabbled. 'They're worse than a crowd of Everton supporters!'

Melinda took in the advancing mob.

'Melinda – Monty – Melanie Beeston!' The mob roared their confused message.

'Oh no, they're not still going on about that!' Melinda sighed.

''Fraid so.' This time, Carmel prized herself for her quick thinking. First, if she didn't already know it, it was mega important for Melinda not to find out from the fans that Monty was actually here. Second, they had to find a quiet place to explain to her everything that had been going on. Third, she, Carmel Wilde, wanted to be the one who got the celebs back together! 'They're like a pack of wolves,' she warned the DJ.

'Yeah well, they're not having my blood!' Melinda decided, about to turn and run back to her car.

'No, this way!' Carmel suggested, cutting off from the path, across the grass and behind the fountain.

Jade sprinted ahead again, waving her arms like a mad woman. What was Carmel doing, dragging Melinda towards the miniature railway? Didn't she have a brain? 'The other way!' she screeched.

Carmel and Melinda veered sideways, then were driven back again by the crowd.

'Stupid, she'll see Monty!' Jade hissed at Carmel.

Melinda pricked up her ears. 'What did she say about Monty?'

'Nothing!' Carmel skimmed over the question, taking Melinda down past the Pirate Ship and the Musical Horses, past the kiddy rides. 'I think she said Monty loves you!' she announced daringly, pausing for breath beside the Dodgems.

Jade pounced and dragged Melinda and Carmel into a dodgem car, slammed her foot down on the pedal and sped across the metal floor. The car sparked, then careered like a rickety tub away from the noisy fans.

'Come back!' Red Top wailed. 'Have we got news for you!'

'OK, so what does Buggles look like?' Monty asked Deanne as they stood on the platform while the mini train steamed into the station.

Choo-choo! Hiss! The train was red and black, its wheels polished steel.

'He's got a green face, no hair and four arms,' Deanne explained. But her answer was lost in the whistle and hiss of the train.

'Get in!' Krystal urged, ignoring the station master in his striped shirt and dark blue waistcoat, trying to make them form a queue. At least they'd got away from the crowd, thanks to Deanne.

Monty looked out at the neat yellow flowers in smart tubs which lined the platform. 'Did you say he's wearing a green fleece, with short hair and he lives on a farm?'

'Yes!' Kayleigh cut in.

'He likes chocolate,' Deanne added.

Crash! Jade's dodgem car collided with a pole. Sparks flew and metal scraped.

'Monty's here!' Red Top screeched.

Melinda jumped out the car minus one shoe. 'What did that kid just say?' she demanded, hobbling on one high heel.

Jade and Carmel ran after her. 'Wait, Melinda!' they cried. 'OK, Monty did show up in the end, but we need to talk to you about it!'

'When? Where?' Totally thrown off-guard, the DJ wandered away from the dodgems towards the track of the miniature railway.

Choo-choo! The tiny train was approaching in a cloud of steam.

'Watch out!' Carmel cried.

Chug-chug! A dazed Melinda stopped to let the train go by. She looked up at the gleaming red engine and the open carriages full of happy, waving passengers.

'Mel!' a voice yelled.

As the steam cleared, she looked again at a crazy guy half-hanging out of the train, his blond hair blown back from his face, both arms stretched towards her.

'Monty!' she shouted.

'Don't go away!' he cried.

The train chugged by, leaving Melinda standing on the grass in one shoe with her mouth wide open. 'M-M-Monty!' she said again.

Then she turned on Carmel and Jade. 'Come with me,' she ordered. 'I need you two to witness what I have to say to Monty Del Sarto!'

It was Krystal who came running to meet Melinda, Carmel and Jade to tell them that Monty was in a tiny waiting room inside the miniature station.

'The station master said Monty could wait for you in the place where he has his tea breaks,' she explained quickly. 'Monty had to sign his mug with a felt-tip pen.'

...ed up his blue eyes and read ...message on the tiny screen. '"I luv u – Monty"!'

'Hah!' Krystal let out a little yelp of triumph.

'Four words – I love you too!' Melinda sighed, folding her arms around Monty's neck and kissing him in front of everyone.

Click! Simon had snapped the moment.

Kayleigh had hugged Krystal. Carmel had beamed at Jade. Deanne had been busy scolding Buggle-mug.

'Don't ever run off like that again!' she'd told him. 'And it's no good trying to pretend that you weren't lost, because I know you were!'

She'd found the runaway hiding in the waiting room, eating the station master's KitKats. He hadn't even been sorry for nearly ruining her day.

Give me a hug! he'd telepathed.

And she'd forgiven him at the moment when Melinda had murmured 'I love you too!'

''Course, it's down to me,' Krystal claimed now. She'd cornered Simon and asked him why he'd been snapping away.

'These pictures are worth a fortune to *Hi!* magazine,' he'd replied. 'This is the biggest story to hit the music world this year, and I happen to be the only person around to take the photographs.'

Krystal had quickly seized the point. 'You're gonna earn money out of this?'

'Thousands,' Simon had assured her, tapping his camera.

'I sent that text message to Melinda!' she reminded the budding photo-journalist.

Her sisters gathered round while Monty and Melinda emerged hand in hand on to the station platform.

The crowd of fans had caught up. They were cheering the reunited couple.

Yeah, Krystal got them back together!' Kayleigh confirmed, looking out over Sundown, feeling that the tricky day was reaching a perfect end.

Click! Simon took a picture of Kayleigh, Krystal, Carmel, Jade and Deanne Wilde with their arms linked, grinning at the camera.

'Smile, Buggle-mug!' Deanne said under her breath.

'Yeah, say cheese!' even Jade agreed.